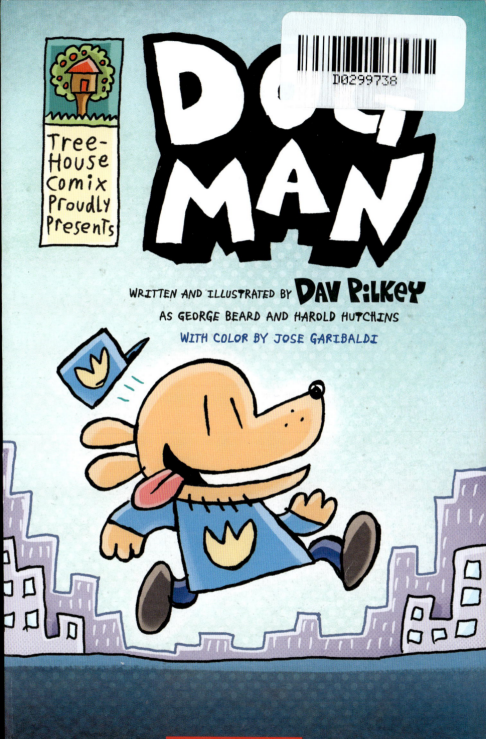

For Dan, Leah, Alek, and Kyle Santat

Published in the UK by Scholastic, 2017
Euston House, 24 Eversholt Street, London, NW1 1DB
Scholastic Ireland, 89E Lagan Road, Dublin Industrial Estate,
Glasnevin, Dublin, D11 HP5F

SCHOLASTIC and associated logos are trademarks
and/or registered trademarks of Scholastic Inc.

First published in the US by Scholastic Inc., 2016

Text and illustrations © Dav Pilkey, 2016

The right of Dav Pilkey to be identified as the author and illustrator
of this work has been asserted by him under the Copyright, Designs
and Patents Act 1988.

ISBN 978 1407 14039 1

A CIP catalogue record for this book is available from the British Library.

Printed by Bell & Bain Ltd, Glasgow
Paper made from wood grown in sustainable forests
and other controlled sources.

29

www.scholastic.co.uk

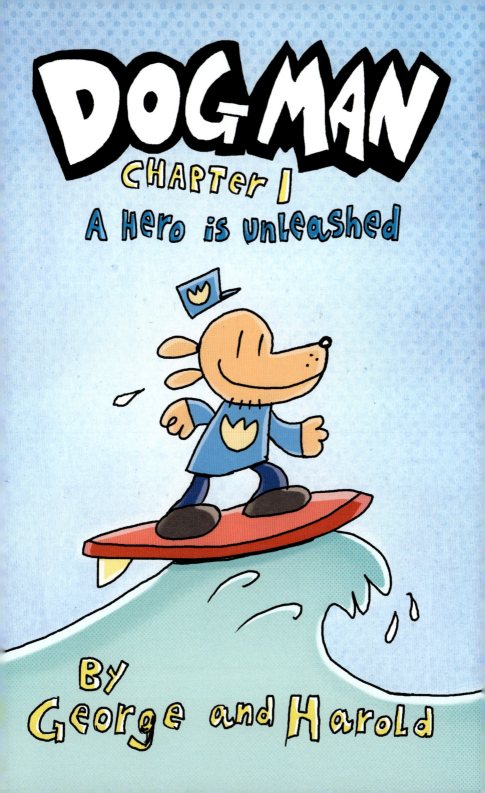

16

And soon, a brand-new crime-fighting sensation ~~sensation~~ was unleashed.

HooRay For Dog Man!

The news spread Quickly!

CITY NEWS

Dog Man is World's greatest Cop!!!!!

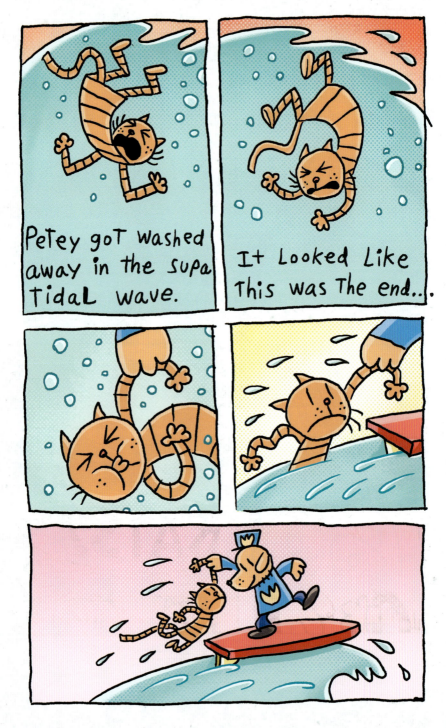

Petey got washed away in the supa tidal wave.

It looked like this was the end...

The Tidal wave got smaller and smaller...

...until it ended at Just the right Spot.

HEY COPS!!! Dog man captured Petey!!

This calls for a celebration!!!

Remember, Flip only page 43. Be sure you can see the picture on page 43 **AND** the one on page 45 while you Flip.

Left hand here.

For he's a
jolly good
doggy!

Right
Thumb
here.

For he's a
JoLLy good
doggy!

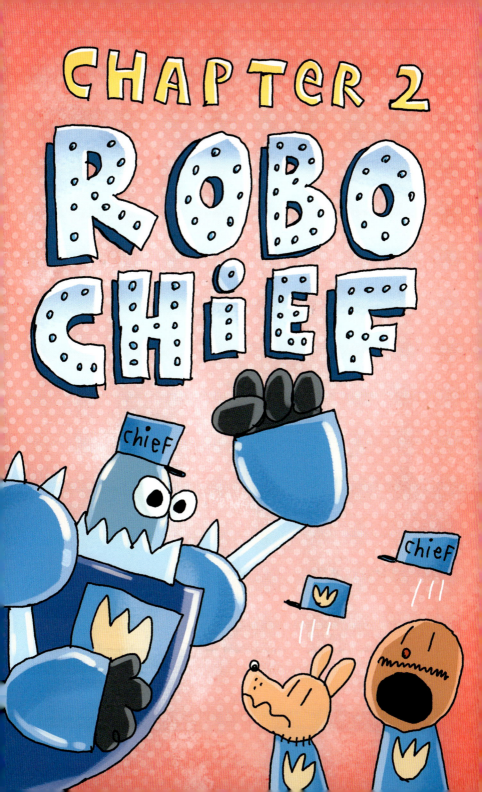

54

Lick

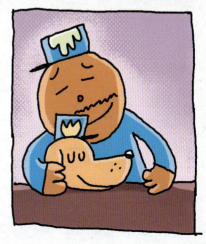

Suddenly, Dog Man's supa ears heard something.

...he rushed to the window...

Soon, my ~~real~~ evil plan will become reality.

Haw Haw Haw!

mayor

soon, Petey walked out of cat Jail.

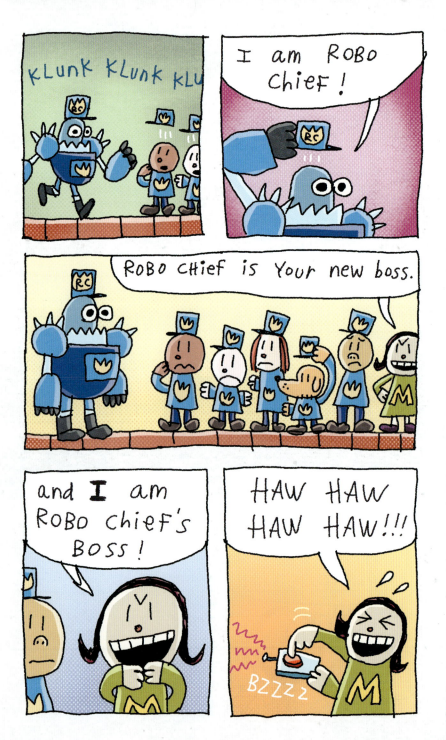

and all cops were ordered to stay away.

Don't go near the mayor's new stores or you will Be Fired!!!

it was the perfect crime...

HAW! HAW! HAW!

...except For one thing!

Hey!

Look at all oF those Rotten stores!

Hackers "R" US

SUPA SCAM

Invisible Petey was not Happy!
Grrr!
Somebody is trying to muscle in on MY Territory!
I have to Stop those evil Jerks!
There can only be ONE villain in this town!!!
Invisible Petey got right to work.
He Followed each customer into the rotten stores...
BILL'S BOMBS

what
goes
up...

... must
come
down

... and
then
back
up
again.

Right
Thumb
here.

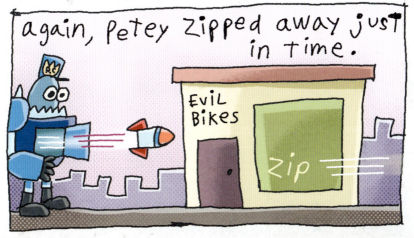

again, Petey zipped away just in time.

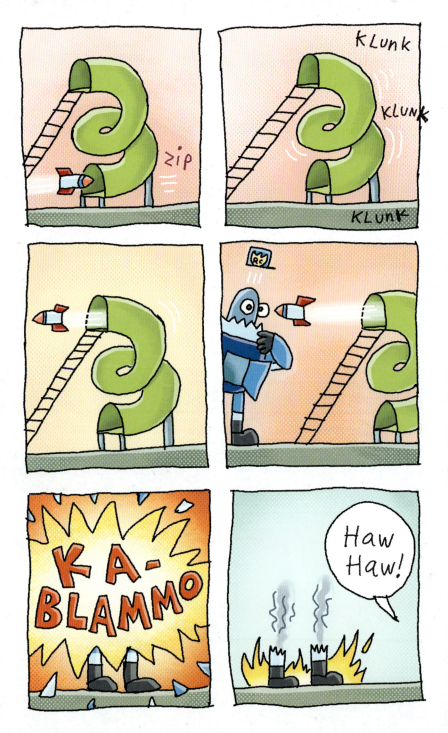

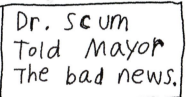

Dr. Scum Told Mayor The bad news.

DOG MAN!

YOU MUST STOP INVISIBLE PETEY!

USE YOUR DOG NOSE TO SNIFF HIM OUT.

GO GET HIM!

Dog Man ran to town.

Sniff Sniff Sniff

Dog Man chased Invisible Petey all over Town...

CHOMP!

...but Invisible Petey was just too quick.

Haw Haw!

DoG Man ran To a nearby Kiddie Pool...

...and dived right in.

SPLASH

DoG Man was aLL weT.

Now it was time to dry off.

FLIP-O-RAMA

Left hand here.

Supa
Soaker

99

Right
Thumb
here.

Supa
Soaker

CHOMP!

where's he going?

Beats me!

Everybody chased Dog Man across Town.

...until...

EX-
Chief's House

So Chief got his old job back...

and soon, everything was back to normal.

Hey!!!

CHAPTER 3

Jerome Horwitz Elementary School

We put the "ow" in Knowledge

Dear Mr. and Mrs. Beard,

Once again I am writing to inform you of your son's disruptive activity in my classroom.

The assignment was to create a WRITTEN public service message to promote reading. Your son and his friend, Harold Hutchins (I am sending a nearly identical letter to Harold's mother), were specifically told NOT to make a comic book for this assignment.

As usual, they did exactly what they were told not to do (see attached comic book). When I confronted George about his disobedience, he claimed that this was not a comic book, but a "graphic novella." I am getting fed up with George's impudence.

I have told both boys on numerous occasions that the classroom is no place for creativity, yet they continue to make these obnoxious and offensive "comix." As you will see, this comic book contains multiple references to human and/or animal feces. It also features a very questionable scene of disregard for homeless/hungry individuals. There are scenes of smoking, violence, nudity, and don't get me started on the spelling and grammar. Frankly, I found the little trash bag "baby" at the end to be very disturbing. I mean, how is that even possible?!!?

George's silly, disruptive behavior, as well as these increasingly disgusting and scatological comic books, are turning my classroom into a zoo. I have spoken to Principal Krupp about Dog Man on numerous occasions. We both believe that you should consider psychological counseling for your son, or at the very least some kind of behavior modification drug to cure his "creative streak."

Regretfully,

Ms. Construde

Ms. Construde
Grade 1 Teacher

and he hadn't had a bath in ages.

Boy, Did Petey stink!

Petey's secret LAB

meanwhile, Dog man was still trying to Find out who Pooed in the Chief's OFFice.

His main suspect was a apple Tree.

suddenly, DOG man smelled something...

DOG man FOLLOWed the cat smell to Petey's hideout.

Petey's secret Lab

he went inside...

...and found Petey's secret stash of Books.

DOG man started to read...

the swing set smacker

Right Thumb here.

The swing set
smacker

The seesaw
smoosher

Right
Thumb
here.

The Seesaw
Smoosher

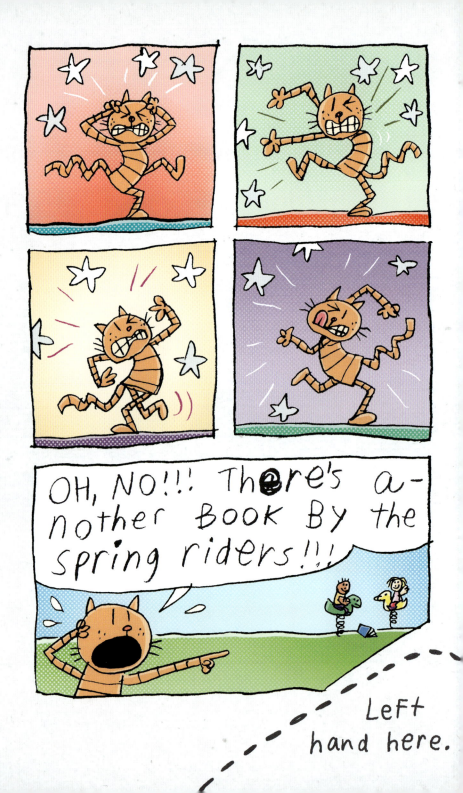

SPRING
Break

Right
Thumb
here.

SPRING
BReak

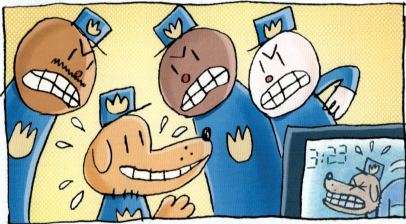

DOG MAN!!!

The end

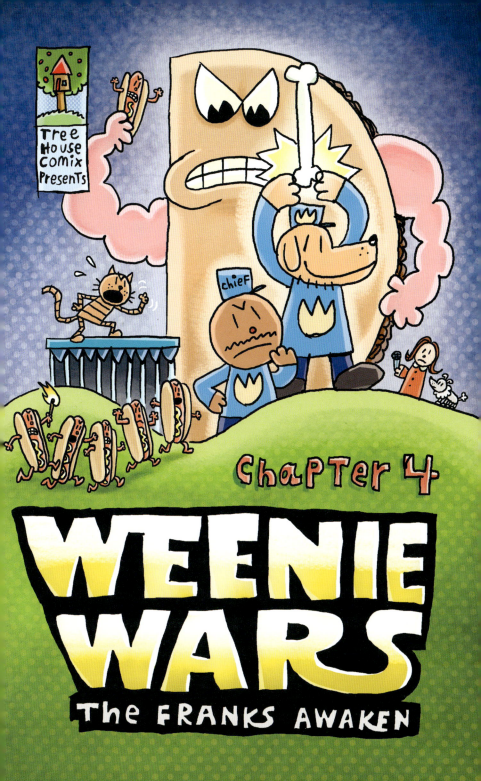

Tree House Comix Presents

chief

CHAPTER 4

WEENIE WARS

THE FRANKS AWAKEN

162

WeLcome

Back,

Chief!

Right
Thumb
here.

It was True! DOG Man was TRapped...

...and all his human STrength didn't help.

OH, NO!!! DOG Man is doomed!

Why was I so mean to him???

There, there, Chief.

DOG Man will save the day! You'll see!

189

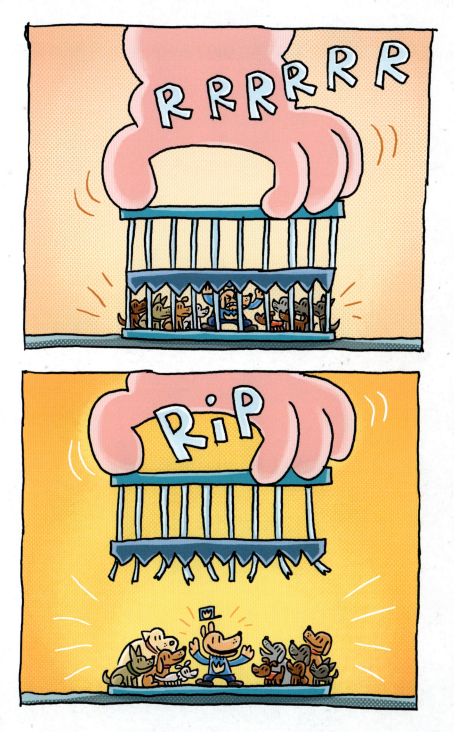

Hip!

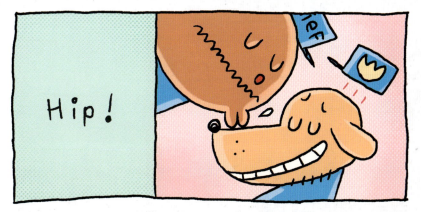

Hip!

Hooray!!!

220

REFOCUS FORM

REDO

Name: _Harold H._
Grade: _1_
Teacher: _Mr. Constitude_

I engaged in unacceptable behavior
by: _# making copies of_
dog man comix in
office

My behavior caused other students and teachers to
feel: _Freak out_

How will my behavior change in the future? _be_
more quieter when
making copies of dog man
comix in office.

I am ready to re-join the classroom. Yes ____ No _X_

Why? _too busy making_
dog man comix

Student signature: _Harold H._

NO DRAWING!

HOW MANY TIMES DO WE HAVE TO TALK ABOUT THIS???

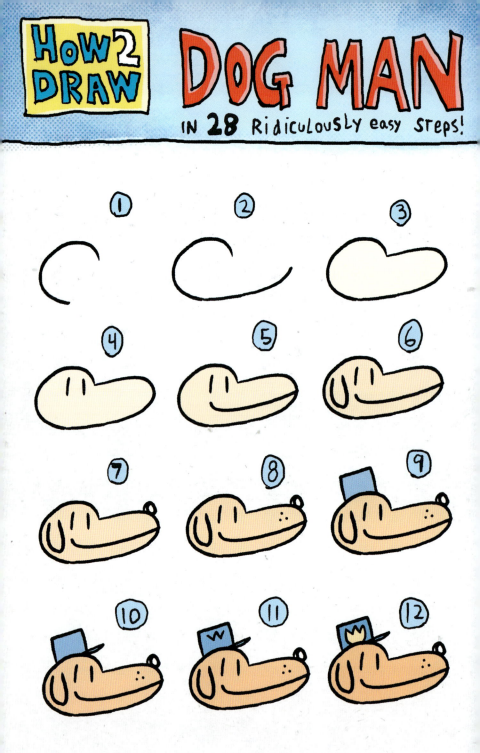

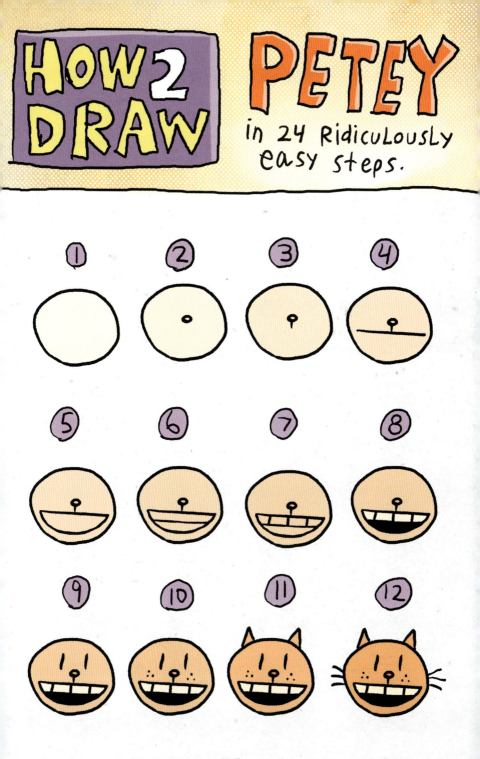

BE EXPRESSIVE

eviL

DiaboLicaL

Supa Sinister

Sad

Angry

Supa angry

Supa, supa
angry

Surprised

Sleepy

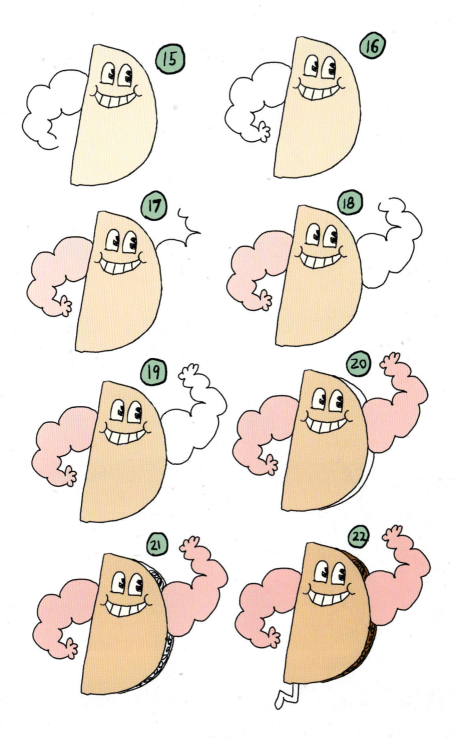

BE EXPRESSIVE!!!

Mad

surprised

Content

Grossed-out

ouch!

Steamed

afraid

Laughing

sleepy

230

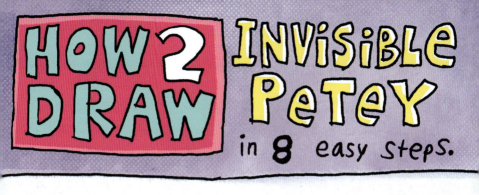
 ① ② ③ ④

⑤ ⑥ ⑦ ⑧

BE EXPRESSIVE!!!

Happy   angry   Sad   oBsequious

ABOUT THE AUTHOR-ILLUSTRATOR

When Dav Pilkey was a kid, he suffered from ADHD, dyslexia, and behavioral problems. Dav was so disruptive in class that his teachers made him sit out in the hall every day. Luckily, Dav loved to draw and make up stories. He spent his time in the hallway creating his own original comic books.

In the second grade, Dav Pilkey created a comic book about a superhero named Captain Underpants. His teacher ripped it up and told him he couldn't spend the rest of his life making silly books.

Fortunately, Dav was not a very good listener.

ABOUT THE COLORIST

Jose Garibaldi grew up on the South Side of Chicago. As a kid, he was a daydreamer and a doodler, and now it's his full-time job to do both. Jose is a professional illustrator, painter, and cartoonist who has created work for Dark Horse Comics, Disney, Nickelodeon, MAD Magazine, and many more. He lives in Los Angeles, California, with his wife and their cats.

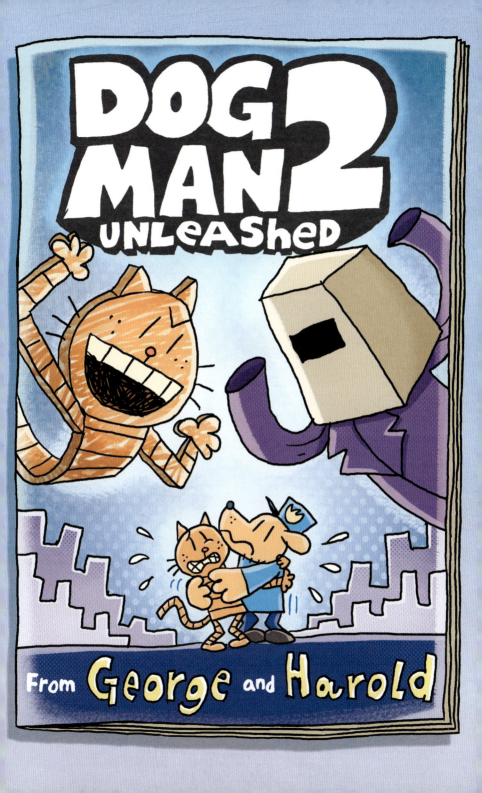